1996

Happy Birthday
Jill

Love
Maureen

BY WELLERAN POLTARNEES

A Most Memorable Birthday

PICTURES BY PAUL CLINE & JUDYTHE SIECK

GREEN TIGER PRESS
Published by Simon & Schuster
New York • London • Toronto • Sydney • Tokyo • Singapore

My Uncle Andrew always sent me wonderful birthday gifts, but the one I received on my seventh birthday was certainly the best one ever.

My party had just begun when a messenger arrived.

"Is this the home of Thomas Quentin Baker?" he asked.

"Yes," I replied. "I'm Tom."

"I have a gift for you from your Uncle Andrew," said the messenger. He then placed a large, beautifully wrapped box on the table, bowed deeply, and left as quickly as he'd come.

My friends and I stared in disbelief as the package began, as if by magic, to unwrap itself.

When all the ribbon and wrapping had fallen away, the side of the box opened, and out stepped what looked for all the world like a tiny ringmaster.

"We are the Great Sparks and Wheeler Traveling Circus," he announced in a small but clear voice. "We have been sent by your Uncle Andrew to give a special birthday performance for his favorite nephew, Thomas. We shall do our best to delight and entertain you and your friends."

"And now, for our final act," proclaimed the ringmaster, "we will march back into our traveling box and rewrap it from the inside. We thank you all for your kind attention, and bid you a fond farewell!"

Again, my friends and I watched in wonder as the circus troupe entered the box which rewrapped itself with a great flourish.

The messenger appeared at the door once more.

"Master Thomas," he said. "I have come to remove the package which your uncle hopes has given you and your guests great pleasure."

And with that he left, and so ended a wonderful birthday which I shall never forget.

GREEN TIGER PRESS, Simon & Schuster Building, Rockefeller Center, 1230 Avenue of the Americas, New York, New York 10020
Text copyright © 1993 by Blue Lantern Studio, Inc.   Illustrations copyright © 1993 by Paul Cline and Judythe Sieck
All rights reserved including the right of reproduction in whole or in part in any form.
GREEN TIGER PRESS is an imprint of Simon & Schuster.
Manufactured in the United States of America
Design & title by Judythe Sieck.

10 9 8 7 6 5 4 3 2 1

Library of Congress Cataloging-in-Publication Data
Poltarnees. Welleran. A most memorable birthday / by Welleran Poltarnees; Illustrated by Paul Cline and Judythe Sieck. p. cm.
Summary: On his birthday Thomas receives a miniature circus troupe from his wonderful uncle.
[1. Birthdays—Fiction. 2. Gifts—Fiction. 3. Circus—Fiction.]
I. Cline, Paul, ill. II. Sieck, Judythe, ill. III. Title.
PZ7.P7694Mo 1993   91-43845
[E]—dc20

ISBN: 0-671-77862-5